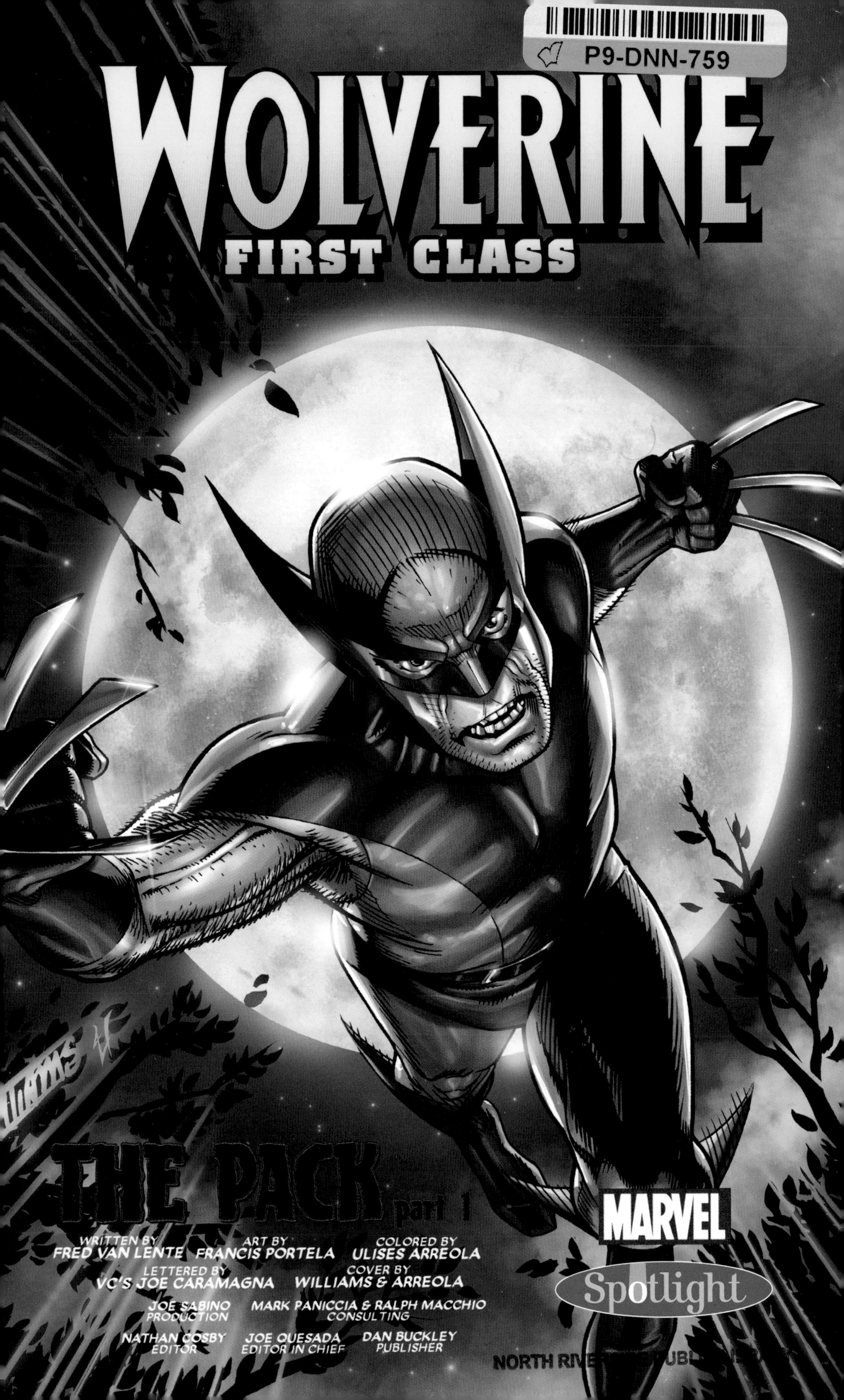
WOLVERINE
FIRST CLASS
THE PACK part 1
WRITTEN BY
FRED VAN LENTE
ART BY
FRANCIS PORTELA
COLORED BY
ULISES ARREOLA
LETTERED BY
VC'S JOE CARAMAGNA
COVER BY
WILLIAMS & ARREOLA
JOE SABINO
PRODUCTION
MARK PANICCIA & RALPH MACCHIO
CONSULTING
NATHAN COSBY
EDITOR
JOE QUESADA
EDITOR IN CHIEF
DAN BUCKLEY
PUBLISHER
MARVEL
Spotlight

Visit us at www.abdopublishing.com

Reinforced library bound editions published in 2014 by Spotlight, a division of the
ABDO Group, PO Box 398166, Minneapolis, MN 55439. Spotlight produces
high-quality reinforced library bound editions for schools and libraries.
Published by agreement with Marvel Characters, Inc.

Printed in the United States of America, North Mankato, Minnesota.
042013
092013
♻ This book contains at least 10% recycled material.

MARVEL

marvel.com
© 2013 Marvel

Library of Congress Cataloging-in-Publication Data

Van Lente, Fred
[Graphic novels. Selections]
 The pack / story by Fred Van Lente ; art by Francis Portela. -- Reinforced library
bound edition.
     volumes cm. -- (Wolverine, first class)
 "Marvel."
 Summary: "Wolverine's claws and healing factor have helped him survive some of
the most dangerous situations and locales. But what happens when dark magic trans-
forms him into a werewolf?"-- Provided by publisher.
 ISBN 978-1-61479-178-2 (part 1) -- ISBN 978-1-61479-179-9 (part 2)
1. Graphic novels. [1. Graphic novels. 2. Superheroes--Fiction.] I. Portela, Francis,
illustrator. II. Title.
PZ7.7.V26Pac 2013
741.5'352--dc23
                                                2013005934

All Spotlight books are reinforced library bindings
and manufactured in the United States of America.

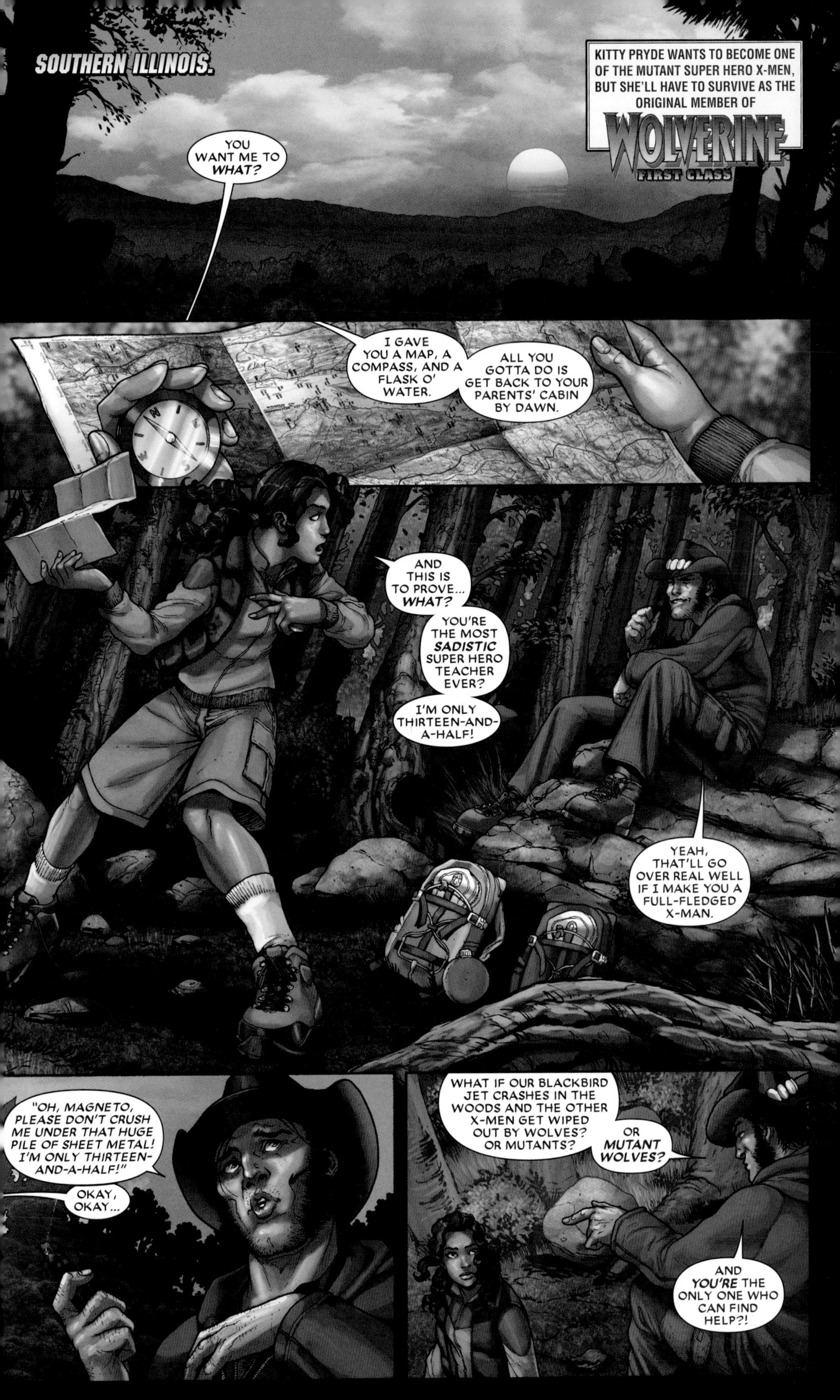
SOUTHERN ILLINOIS.
KITTY PRYDE WANTS TO BECOME ONE OF THE MUTANT SUPER HERO X-MEN, BUT SHE'LL HAVE TO SURVIVE AS THE ORIGINAL MEMBER OF
WOLVERINE FIRST CLASS
YOU WANT ME TO *WHAT?*
I GAVE YOU A MAP, A COMPASS, AND A FLASK O' WATER.
ALL YOU GOTTA DO IS GET BACK TO YOUR PARENTS' CABIN BY DAWN.
AND THIS IS TO PROVE... *WHAT?*
YOU'RE THE MOST *SADISTIC* SUPER HERO TEACHER EVER?
I'M ONLY THIRTEEN-AND-A-HALF!
YEAH, THAT'LL GO OVER REAL WELL IF I MAKE YOU A FULL-FLEDGED X-MAN.
"OH, MAGNETO, PLEASE DON'T CRUSH ME UNDER THAT HUGE PILE OF SHEET METAL! I'M ONLY THIRTEEN-AND-A-HALF!"
OKAY, OKAY...
WHAT IF OUR BLACKBIRD JET CRASHES IN THE WOODS AND THE OTHER X-MEN GET WIPED OUT BY WOLVES? OR MUTANTS?
OR *MUTANT WOLVES?*
AND *YOU'RE* THE ONLY ONE WHO CAN FIND HELP?!

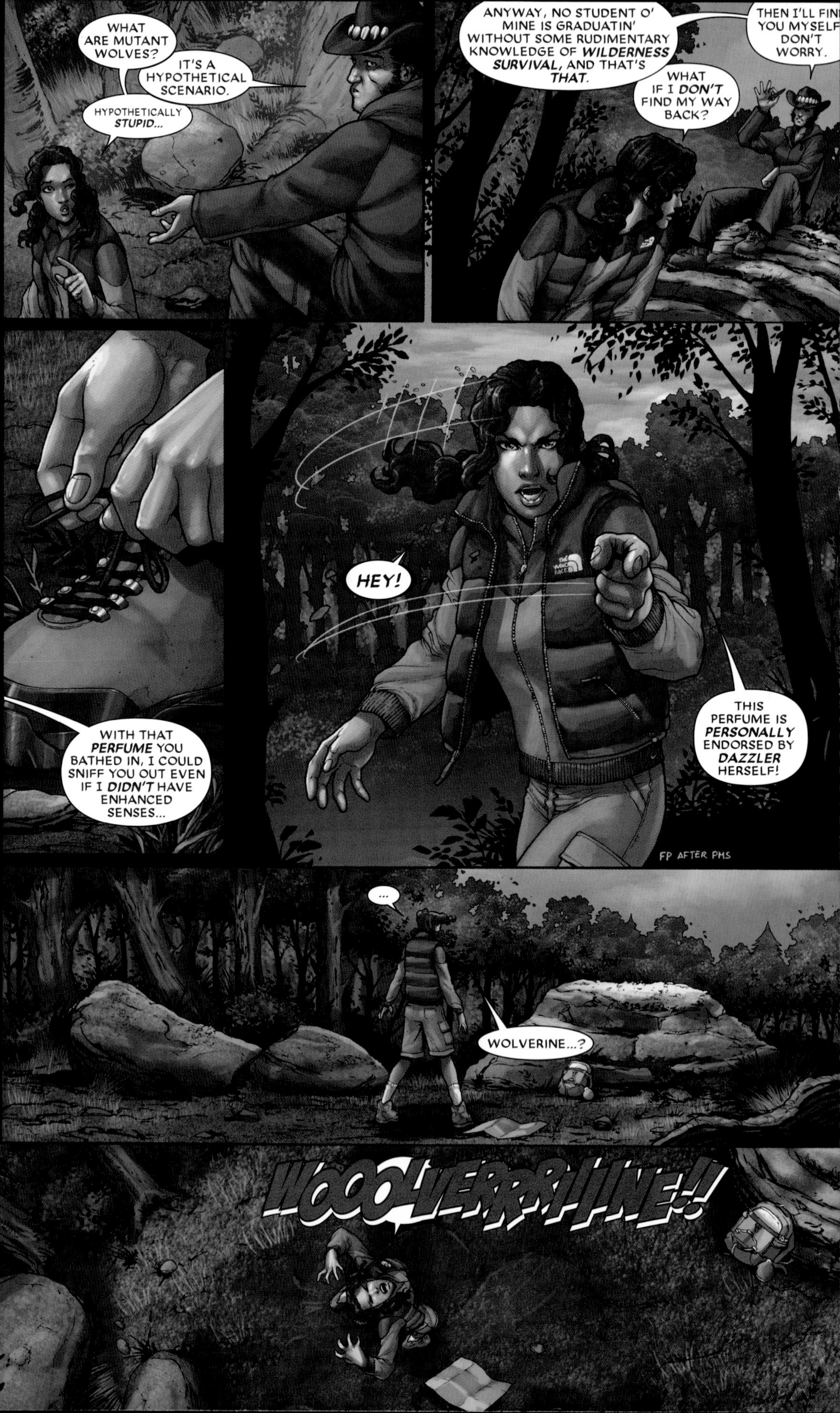
WHAT ARE MUTANT WOLVES?
IT'S A HYPOTHETICAL SCENARIO.
HYPOTHETICALLY *STUPID*...
ANYWAY, NO STUDENT O' MINE IS GRADUATIN' WITHOUT SOME RUDIMENTARY KNOWLEDGE OF *WILDERNESS SURVIVAL*, AND THAT'S *THAT*.
WHAT IF I *DON'T* FIND MY WAY BACK?
THEN I'LL FIND YOU MYSELF. DON'T WORRY.
WITH THAT *PERFUME* YOU BATHED IN, I COULD SNIFF YOU OUT EVEN IF I *DIDN'T* HAVE ENHANCED SENSES...
HEY!
THIS PERFUME IS *PERSONALLY* ENDORSED BY *DAZZLER* HERSELF!
FP AFTER PHS
...
WOLVERINE...?
WOOOLVERRRIIINE!!

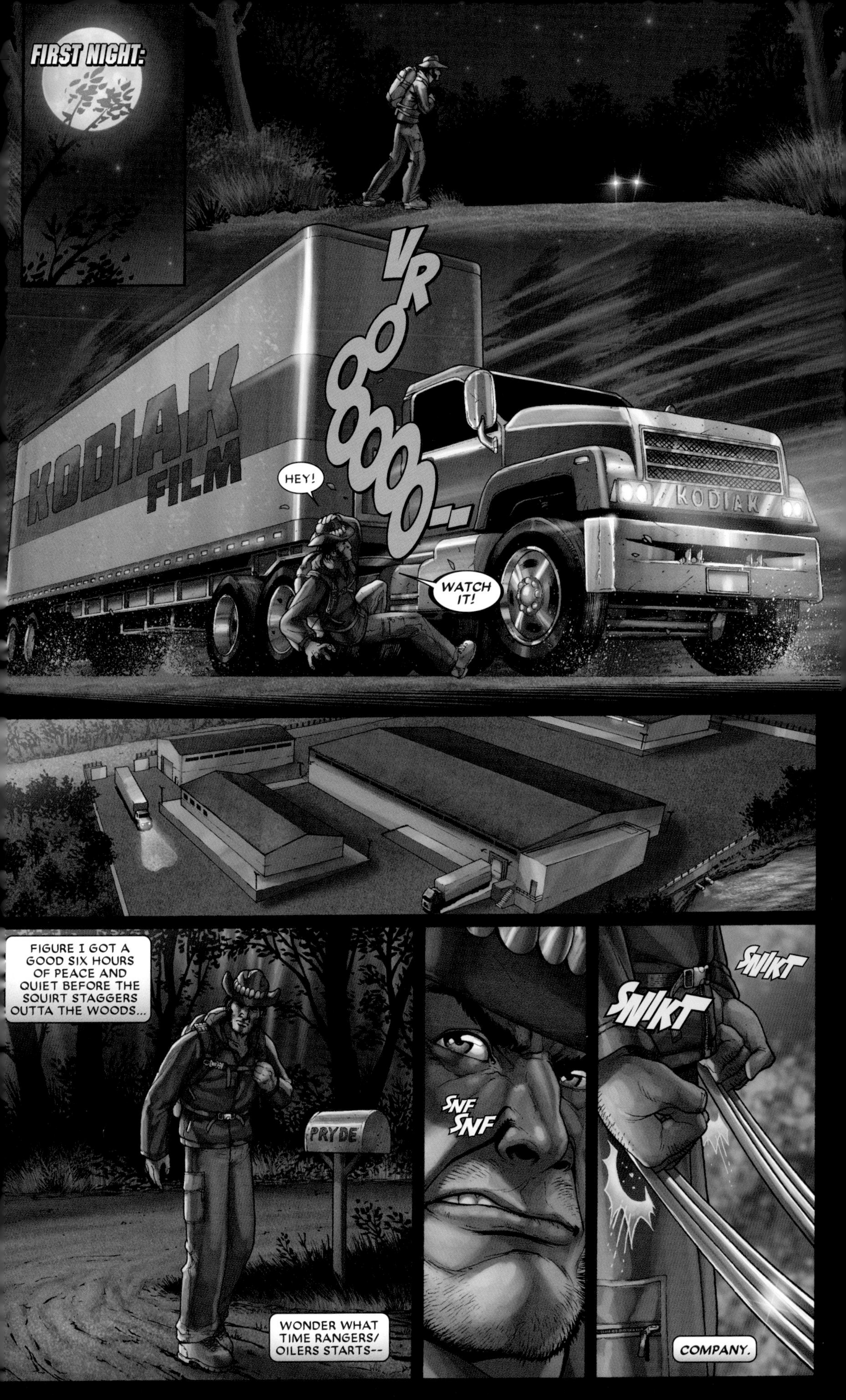
FIRST NIGHT:
VROOOOOO
HEY!
WATCH IT!
KODIAK FILM
KODIAK
FIGURE I GOT A GOOD SIX HOURS OF PEACE AND QUIET BEFORE THE SQUIRT STAGGERS OUTTA THE WOODS...
PRYDE
WONDER WHAT TIME RANGERS/ OILERS STARTS--
SNF SNF
SNIKT
SNIKT
COMPANY.

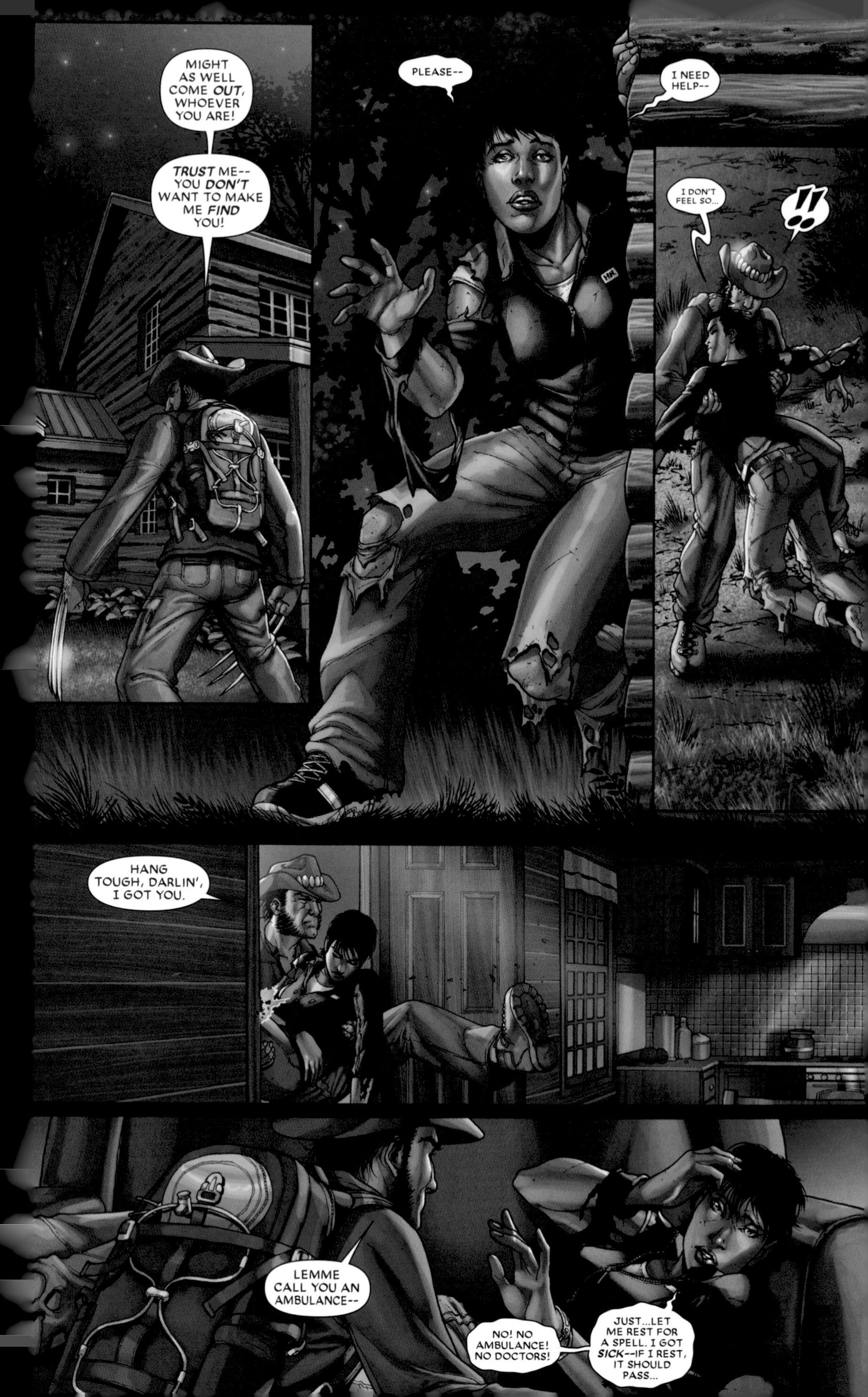
MIGHT AS WELL COME OUT, WHOEVER YOU ARE!
TRUST ME--YOU DON'T WANT TO MAKE ME FIND YOU!
PLEASE--
I NEED HELP--
I DON'T FEEL SO...
!!
HANG TOUGH, DARLIN', I GOT YOU.
LEMME CALL YOU AN AMBULANCE--
NO! NO AMBULANCE! NO DOCTORS!
JUST...LET ME REST FOR A SPELL. I GOT SICK--IF I REST, IT SHOULD PASS...

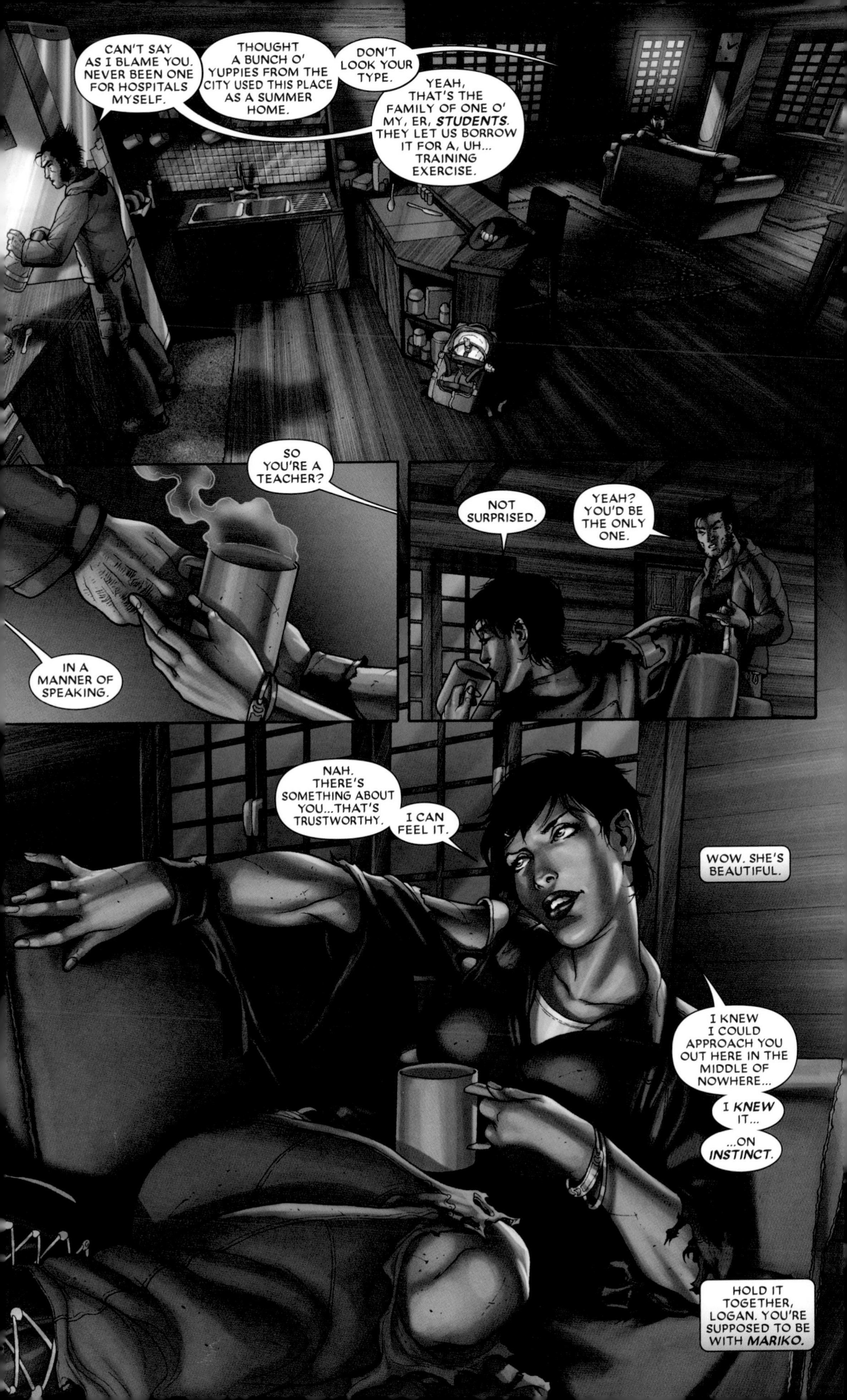
CAN'T SAY AS I BLAME YOU. NEVER BEEN ONE FOR HOSPITALS MYSELF.
THOUGHT A BUNCH O' YUPPIES FROM THE CITY USED THIS PLACE AS A SUMMER HOME.
DON'T LOOK YOUR TYPE.
YEAH, THAT'S THE FAMILY OF ONE O' MY, ER, ***STUDENTS***. THEY LET US BORROW IT FOR A, UH... TRAINING EXERCISE.
SO YOU'RE A TEACHER?
IN A MANNER OF SPEAKING.
NOT SURPRISED.
YEAH? YOU'D BE THE ONLY ONE.
NAH. THERE'S SOMETHING ABOUT YOU...THAT'S TRUSTWORTHY.
I CAN FEEL IT.
WOW. SHE'S BEAUTIFUL.
I KNEW I COULD APPROACH YOU OUT HERE IN THE MIDDLE OF NOWHERE...
I ***KNEW*** IT...
...ON ***INSTINCT***.
HOLD IT TOGETHER, LOGAN. YOU'RE SUPPOSED TO BE WITH ***MARIKO***.

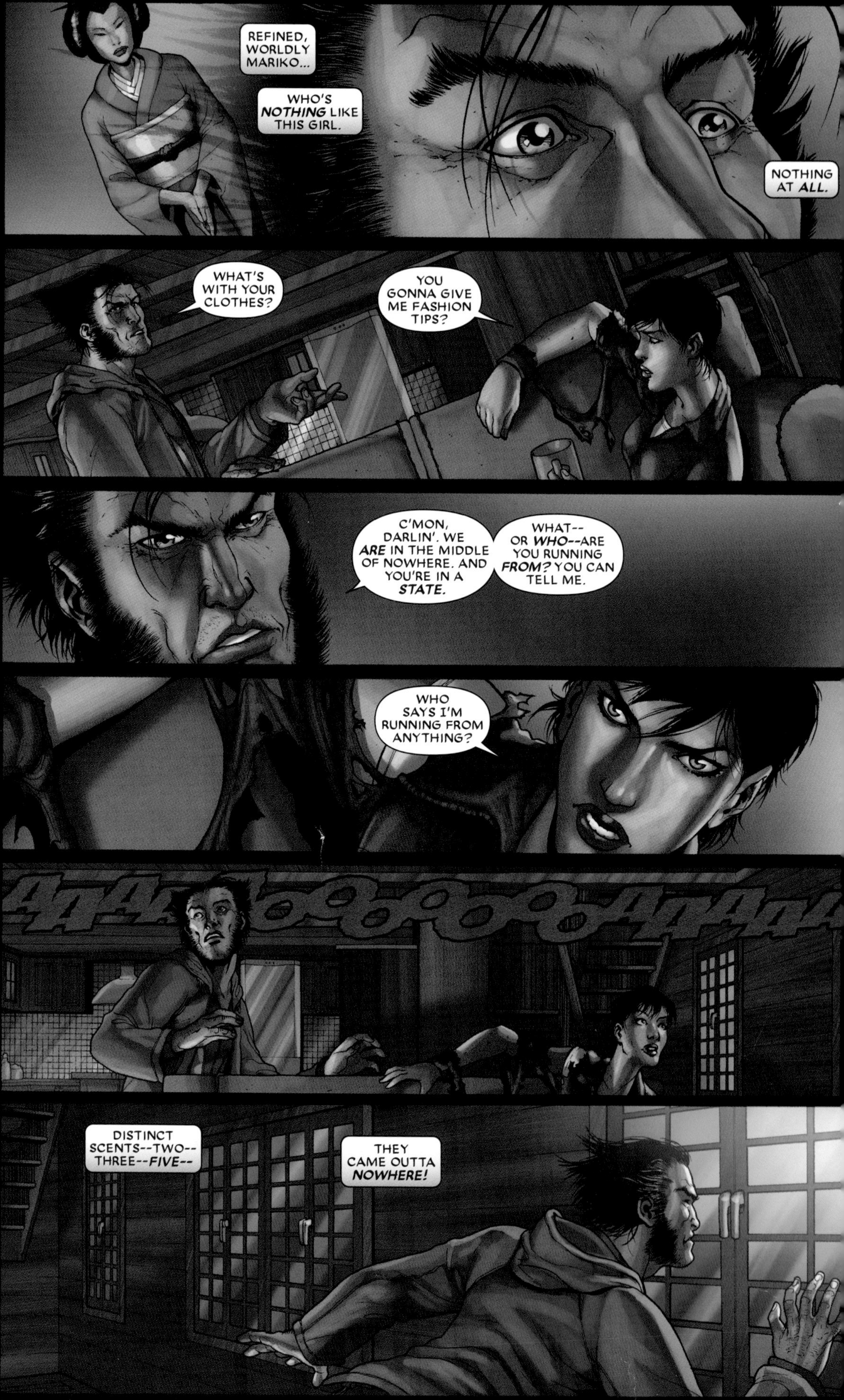
REFINED, WORLDLY MARIKO...
WHO'S NOTHING LIKE THIS GIRL.
NOTHING AT ALL.
WHAT'S WITH YOUR CLOTHES?
YOU GONNA GIVE ME FASHION TIPS?
C'MON, DARLIN'. WE ARE IN THE MIDDLE OF NOWHERE. AND YOU'RE IN A STATE.
WHAT-- OR WHO--ARE YOU RUNNING FROM? YOU CAN TELL ME.
WHO SAYS I'M RUNNING FROM ANYTHING?
DISTINCT SCENTS--TWO--THREE--FIVE--
THEY CAME OUTTA NOWHERE!

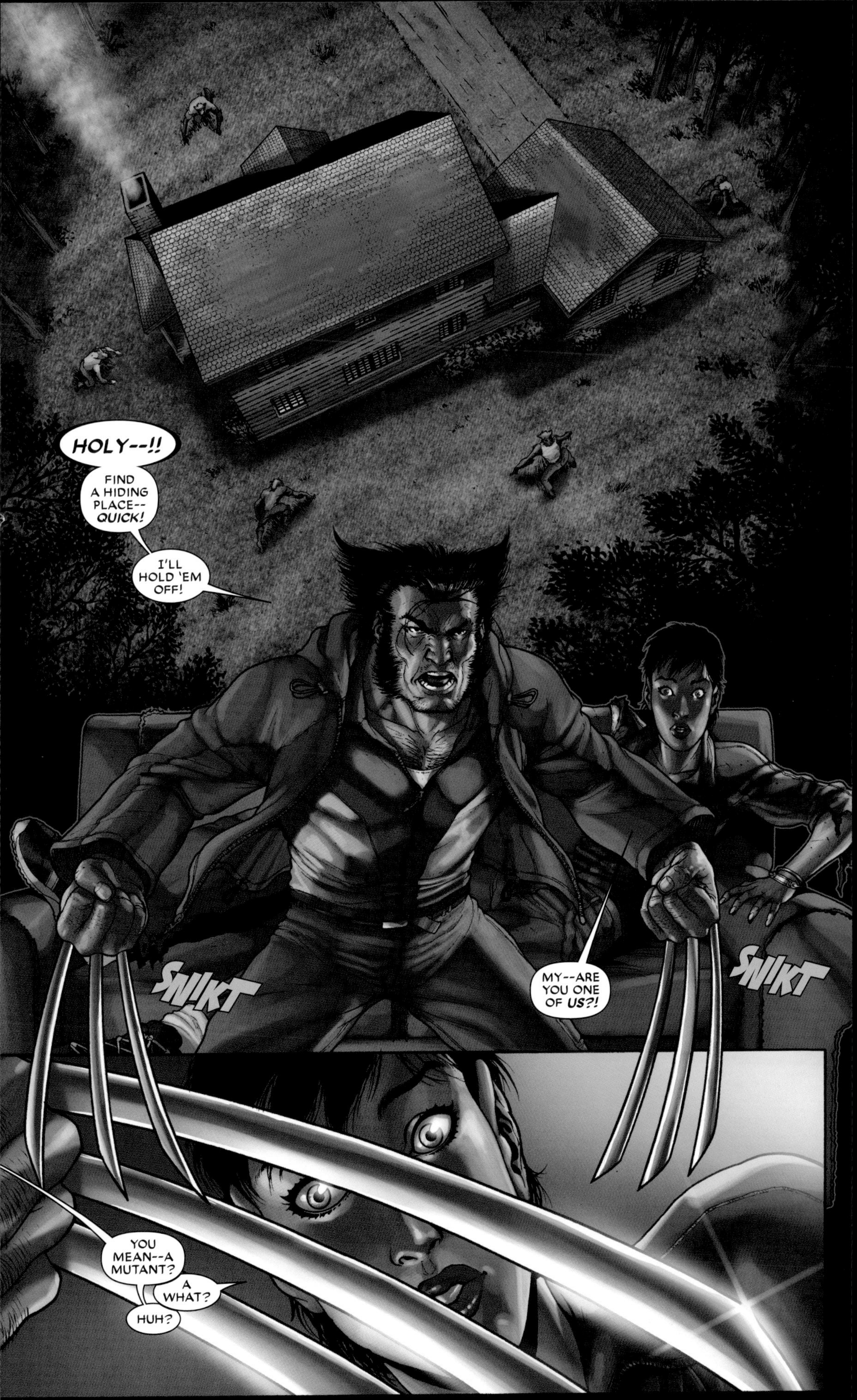
HOLY--!!
FIND A HIDING PLACE--QUICK!
I'LL HOLD 'EM OFF!
SNIKT
MY--ARE YOU ONE OF US?!
SNIKT
YOU MEAN--A MUTANT?
A WHAT?
HUH?

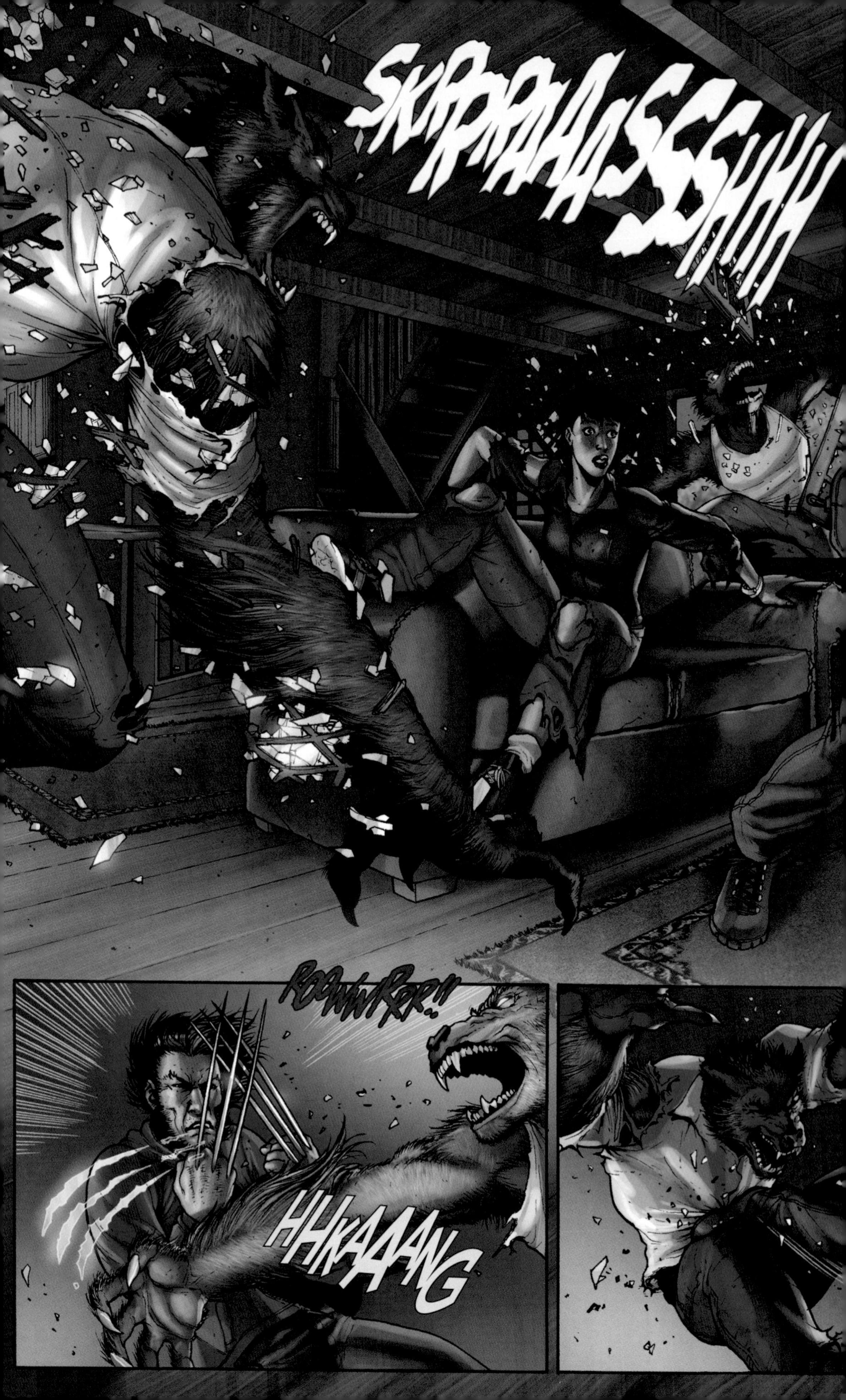
SKRRRAAASSHHH
ROOWWRRR!!
HHKAAANG

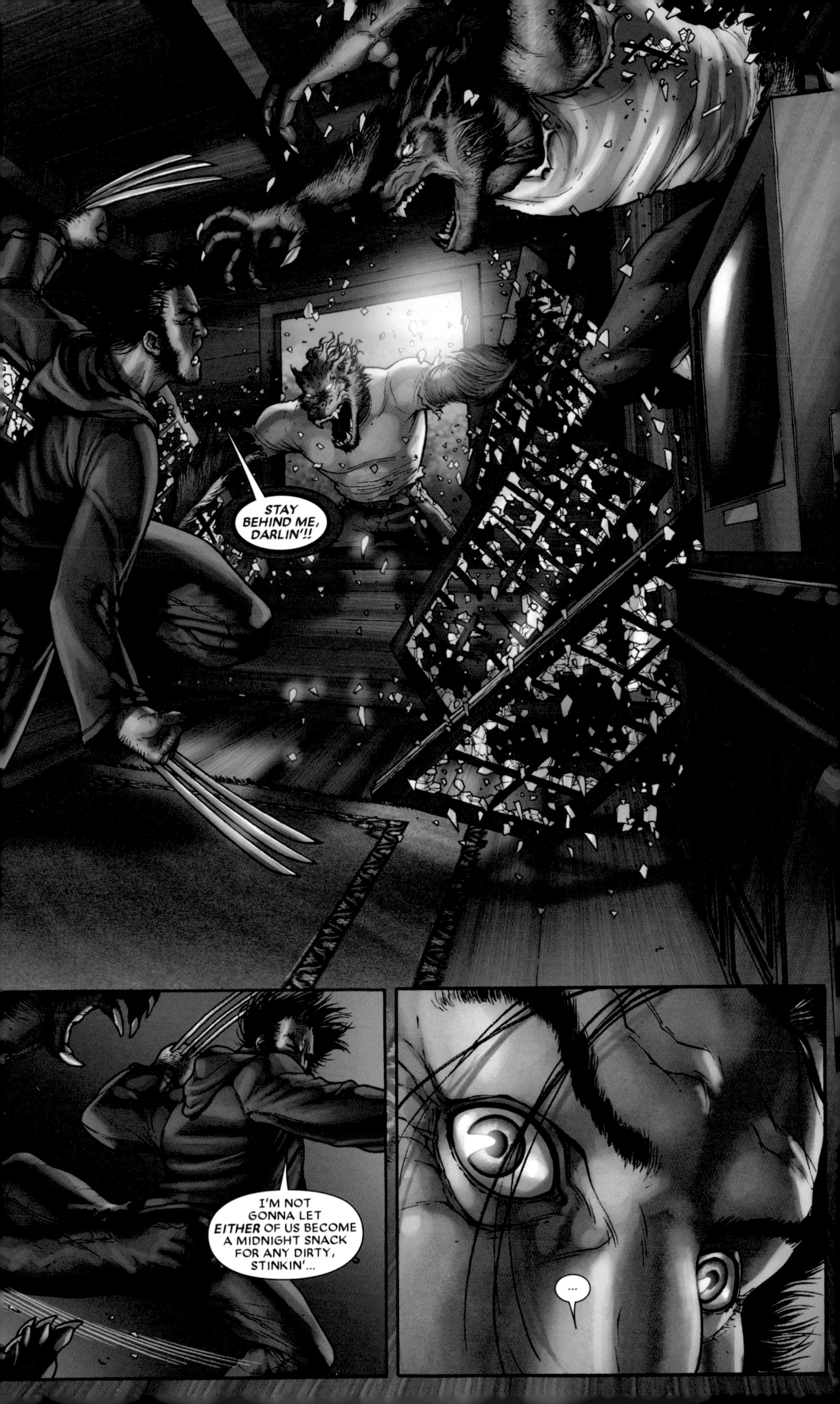
STAY BEHIND ME, DARLIN'!!
I'M NOT GONNA LET EITHER OF US BECOME A MIDNIGHT SNACK FOR ANY DIRTY, STINKIN'...
...

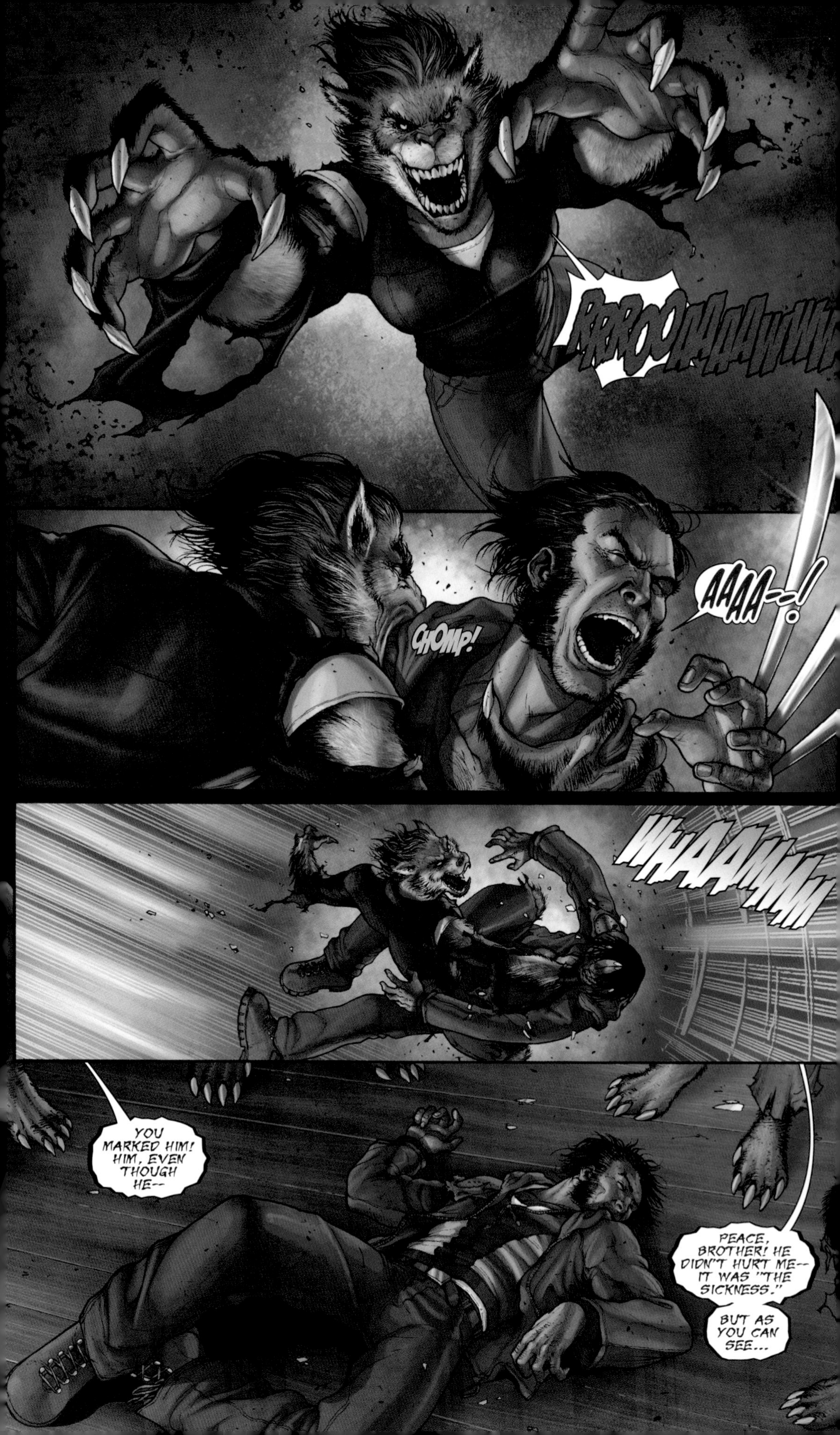
RRROOAAAWWW
CHOMP!
AAAA--!
WHAAMMM
YOU MARKED HIM! HIM, EVEN THOUGH HE--
PEACE, BROTHER! HE DIDN'T HURT ME-- IT WAS "THE SICKNESS."
BUT AS YOU CAN SEE...

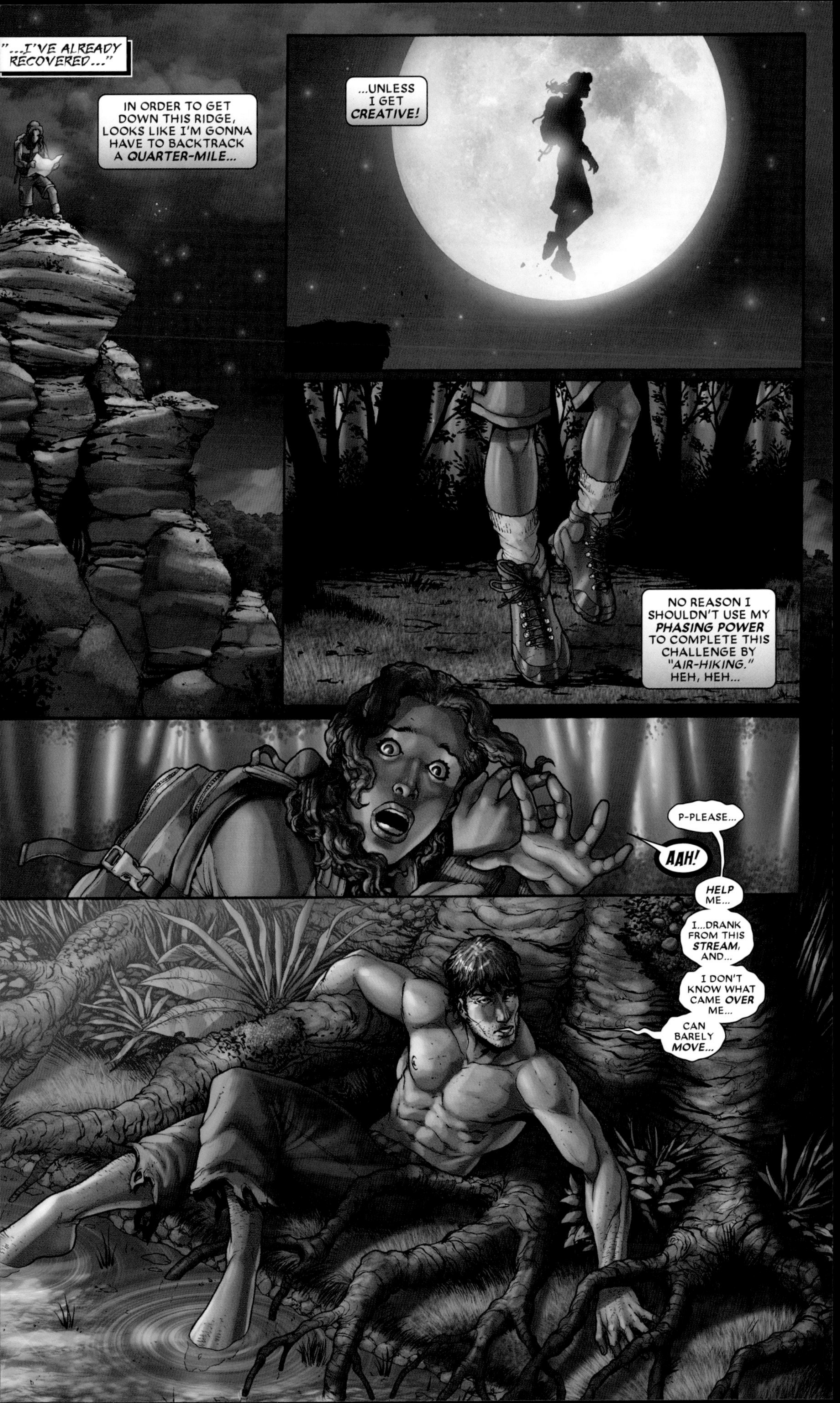

"...I'VE ALREADY RECOVERED..."
IN ORDER TO GET DOWN THIS RIDGE, LOOKS LIKE I'M GONNA HAVE TO BACKTRACK A QUARTER-MILE...
...UNLESS I GET CREATIVE!
NO REASON I SHOULDN'T USE MY PHASING POWER TO COMPLETE THIS CHALLENGE BY "AIR-HIKING." HEH, HEH...
AAH!
P-PLEASE...
HELP ME...
I...DRANK FROM THIS STREAM, AND...
I DON'T KNOW WHAT CAME OVER ME...
CAN BARELY MOVE...

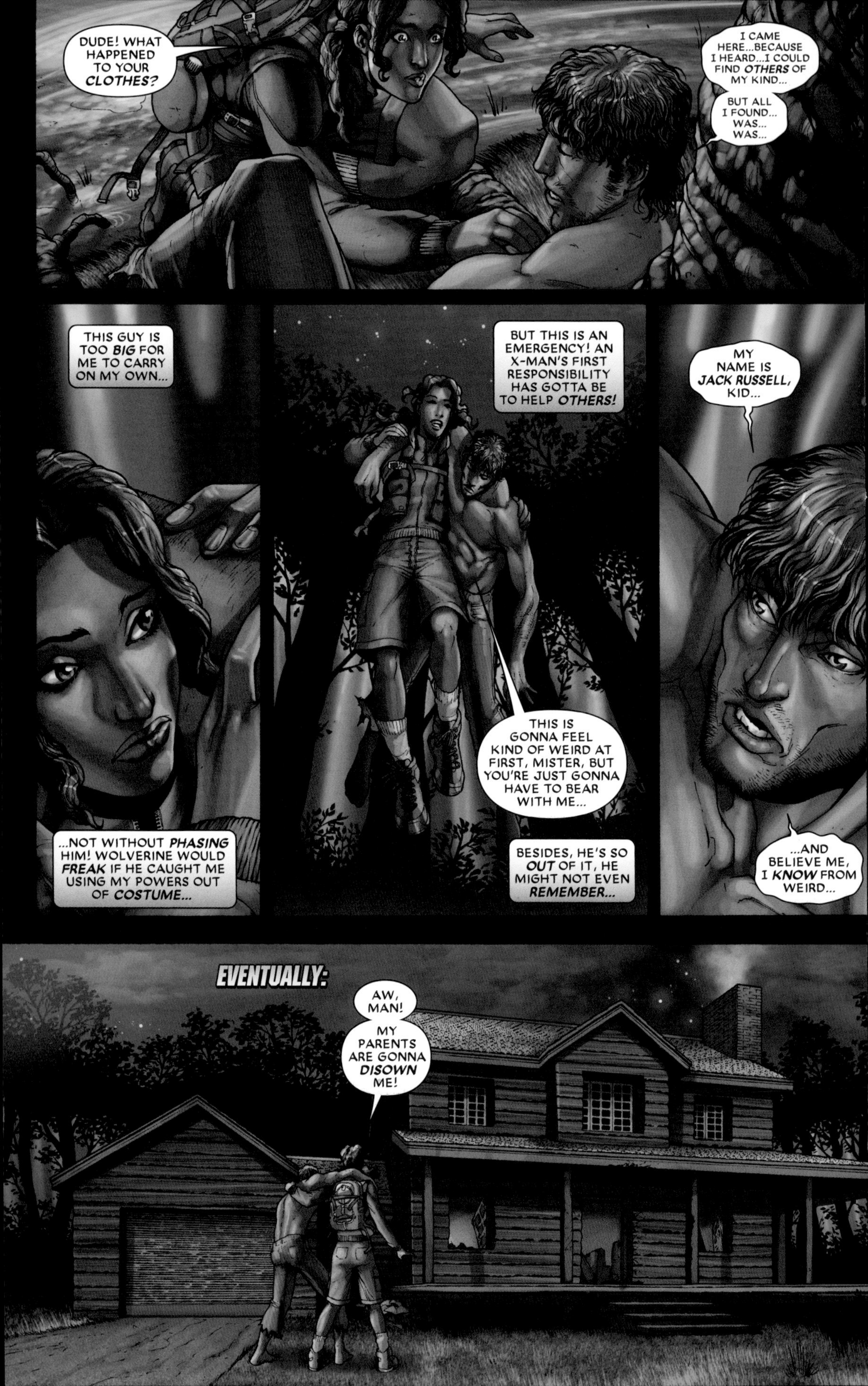
DUDE! WHAT HAPPENED TO YOUR CLOTHES?
I CAME HERE...BECAUSE I HEARD...I COULD FIND OTHERS OF MY KIND...
BUT ALL I FOUND... WAS... WAS...
THIS GUY IS TOO BIG FOR ME TO CARRY ON MY OWN...
...NOT WITHOUT PHASING HIM! WOLVERINE WOULD FREAK IF HE CAUGHT ME USING MY POWERS OUT OF COSTUME...
BUT THIS IS AN EMERGENCY! AN X-MAN'S FIRST RESPONSIBILITY HAS GOTTA BE TO HELP OTHERS!
THIS IS GONNA FEEL KIND OF WEIRD AT FIRST, MISTER, BUT YOU'RE JUST GONNA HAVE TO BEAR WITH ME...
BESIDES, HE'S SO OUT OF IT, HE MIGHT NOT EVEN REMEMBER...
MY NAME IS JACK RUSSELL, KID...
...AND BELIEVE ME, I KNOW FROM WEIRD...
EVENTUALLY:
AW, MAN!
MY PARENTS ARE GONNA DISOWN ME!

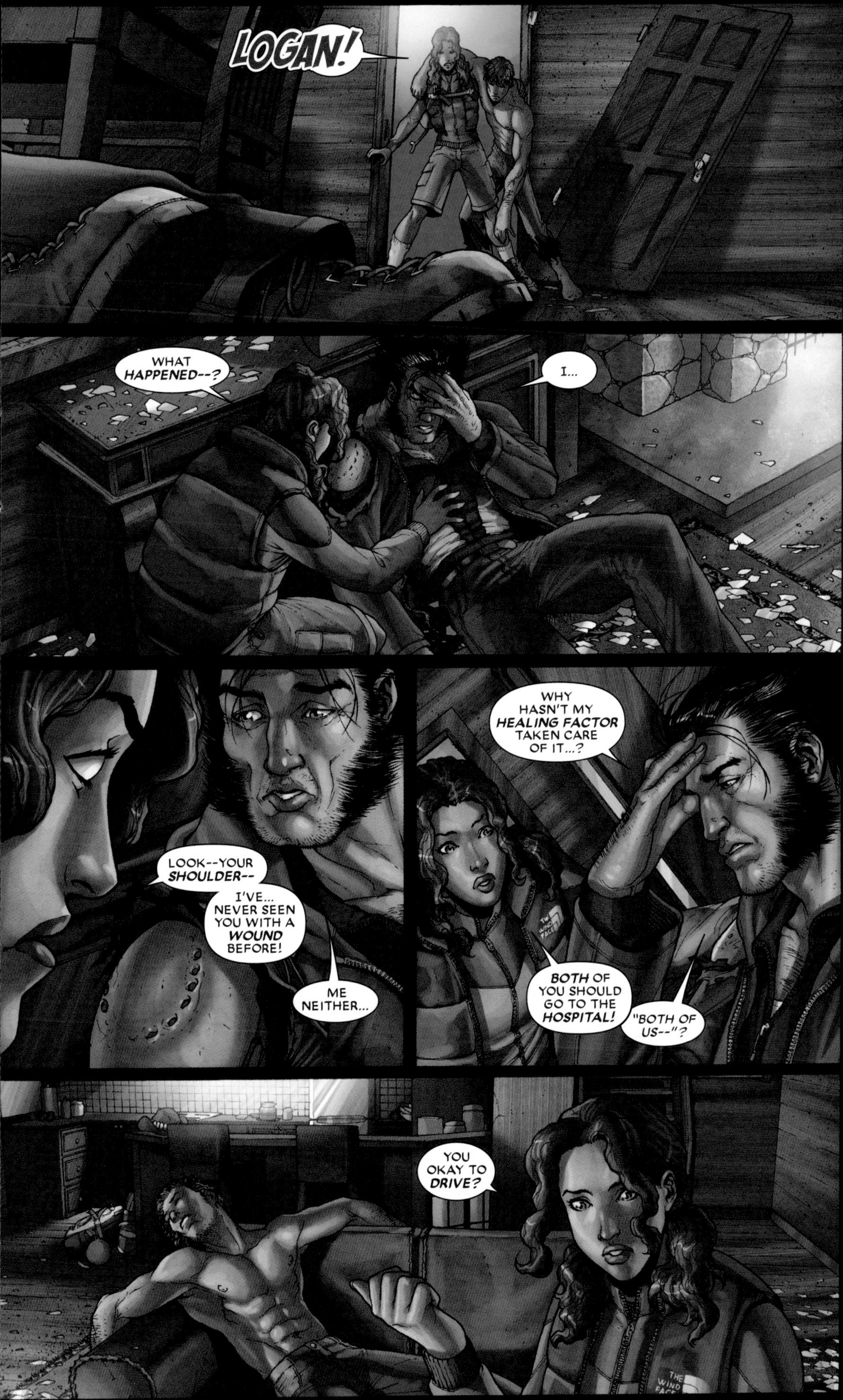
LOGAN!
WHAT HAPPENED--?
I...
LOOK--YOUR SHOULDER--
I'VE... NEVER SEEN YOU WITH A WOUND BEFORE!
ME NEITHER...
WHY HASN'T MY HEALING FACTOR TAKEN CARE OF IT...?
BOTH OF YOU SHOULD GO TO THE HOSPITAL!
"BOTH OF US--"?
YOU OKAY TO DRIVE?

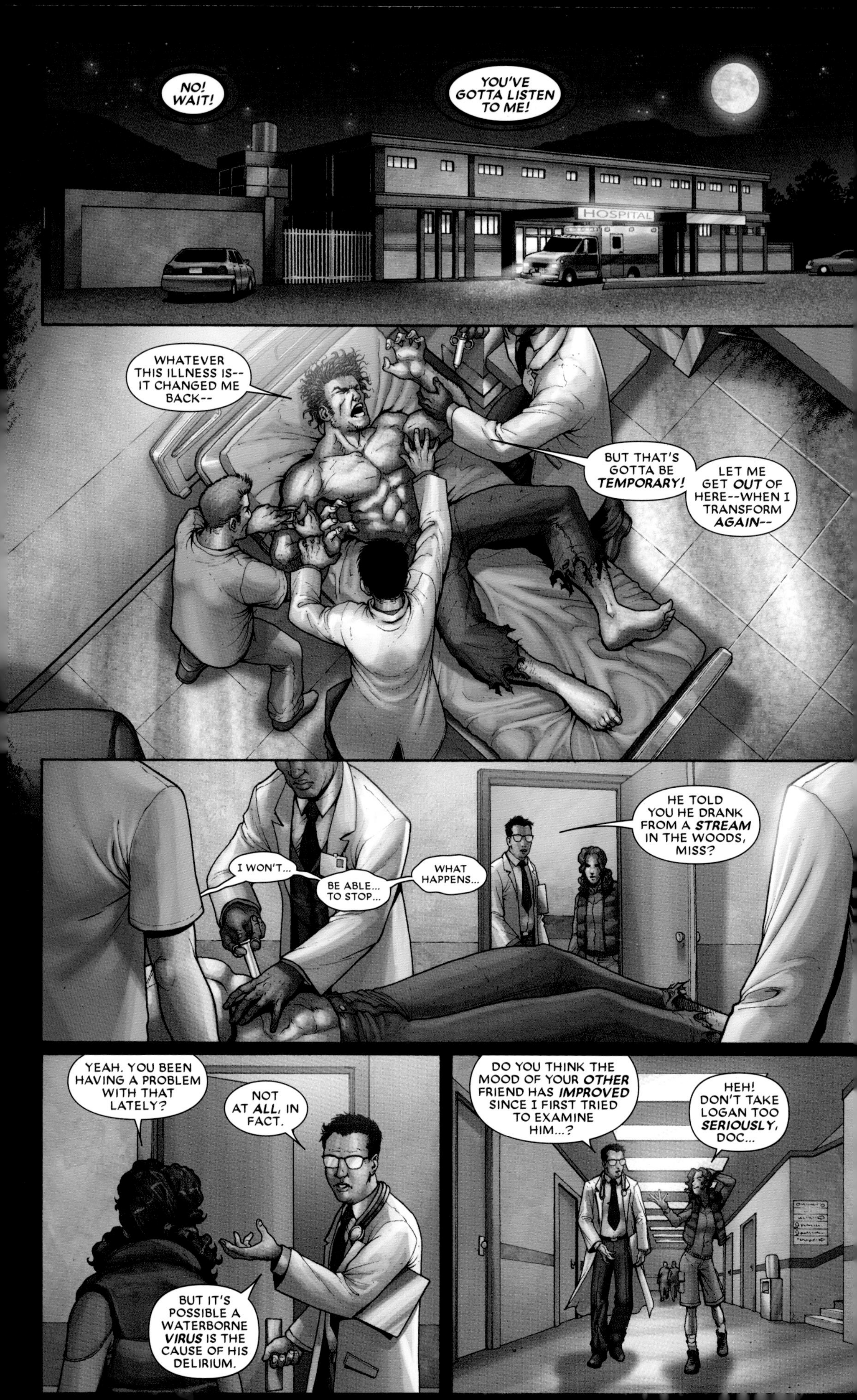
NO! WAIT!
YOU'VE GOTTA LISTEN TO ME!
HOSPITAL
WHATEVER THIS ILLNESS IS-- IT CHANGED ME BACK--
BUT THAT'S GOTTA BE TEMPORARY!
LET ME GET OUT OF HERE--WHEN I TRANSFORM AGAIN--
I WON'T...
BE ABLE... TO STOP...
WHAT HAPPENS...
HE TOLD YOU HE DRANK FROM A STREAM IN THE WOODS, MISS?
YEAH. YOU BEEN HAVING A PROBLEM WITH THAT LATELY?
NOT AT ALL, IN FACT.
BUT IT'S POSSIBLE A WATERBORNE VIRUS IS THE CAUSE OF HIS DELIRIUM.
DO YOU THINK THE MOOD OF YOUR OTHER FRIEND HAS IMPROVED SINCE I FIRST TRIED TO EXAMINE HIM...?
HEH! DON'T TAKE LOGAN TOO SERIOUSLY, DOC...

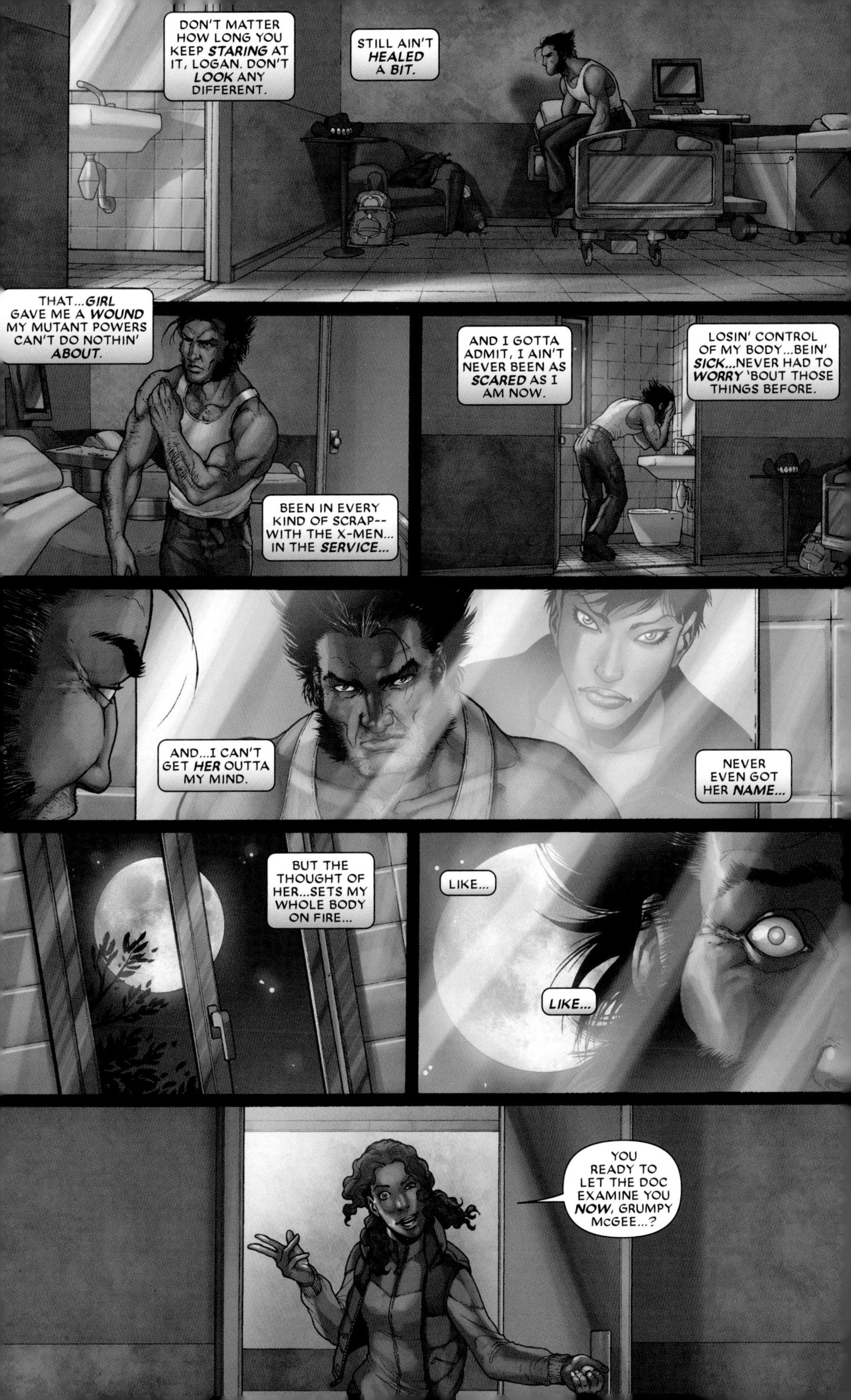

DON'T MATTER HOW LONG YOU KEEP STARING AT IT, LOGAN. DON'T LOOK ANY DIFFERENT.
STILL AIN'T HEALED A BIT.
THAT...GIRL GAVE ME A WOUND MY MUTANT POWERS CAN'T DO NOTHIN' ABOUT.
BEEN IN EVERY KIND OF SCRAP-- WITH THE X-MEN... IN THE SERVICE...
AND I GOTTA ADMIT, I AIN'T NEVER BEEN AS SCARED AS I AM NOW.
LOSIN' CONTROL OF MY BODY...BEIN' SICK...NEVER HAD TO WORRY 'BOUT THOSE THINGS BEFORE.
AND...I CAN'T GET HER OUTTA MY MIND.
NEVER EVEN GOT HER NAME...
BUT THE THOUGHT OF HER...SETS MY WHOLE BODY ON FIRE...
LIKE...
LIKE...
YOU READY TO LET THE DOC EXAMINE YOU NOW, GRUMPY McGEE...?

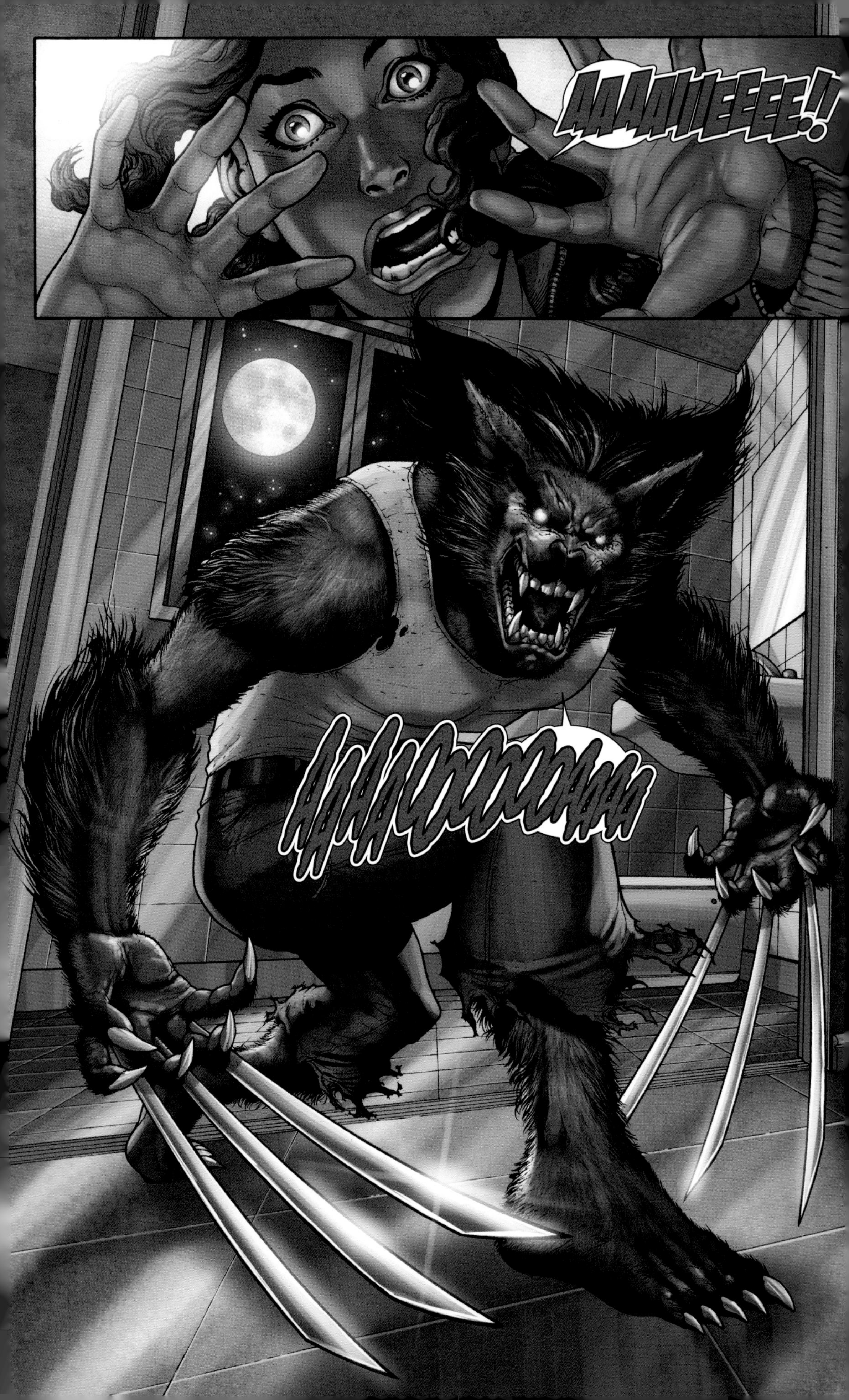
AAAAIIEEEE!!
AAAOOOOOAAAA

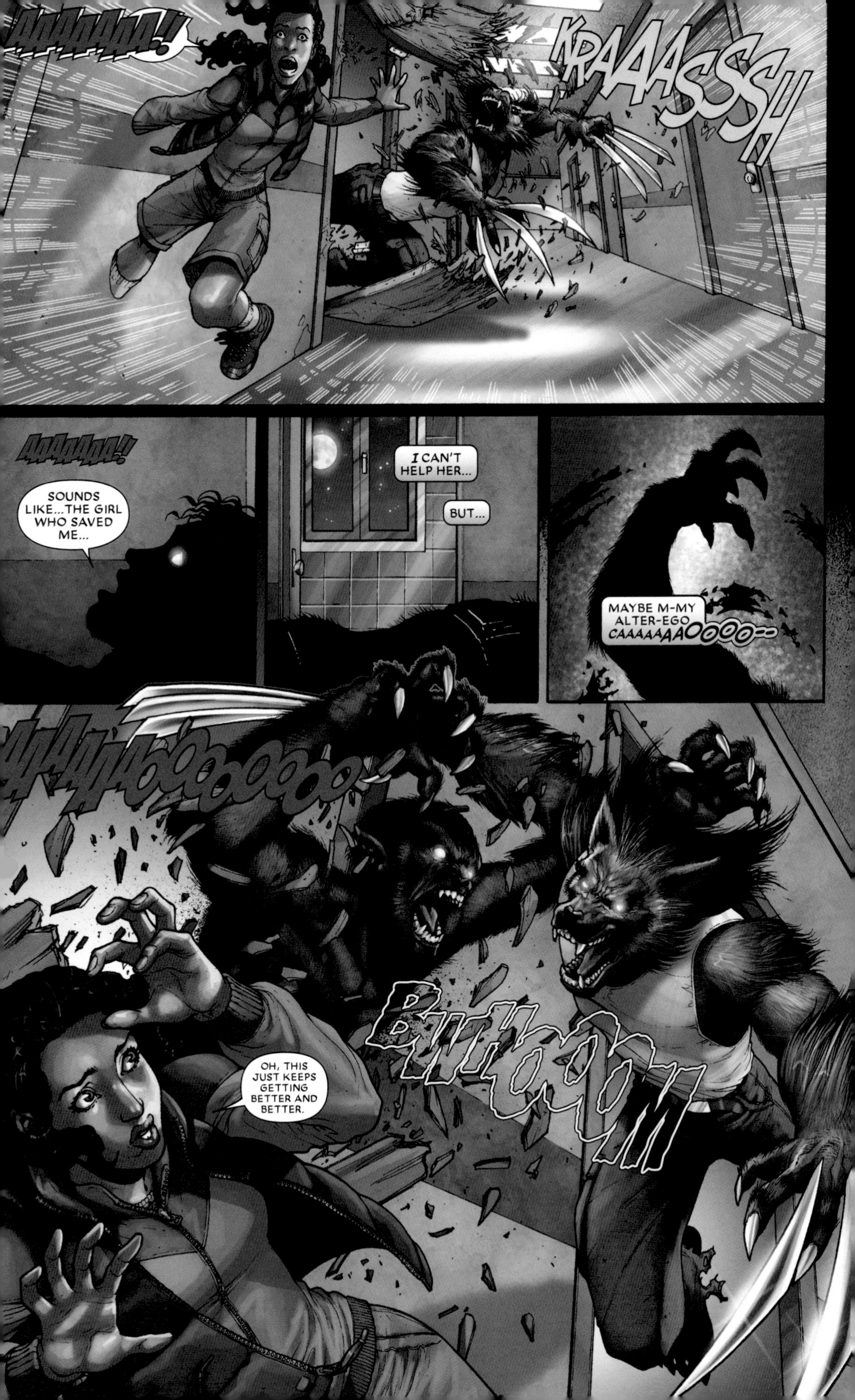
AAAAAAA!!
KRAAASSSH
AAAAAA!!
SOUNDS LIKE...THE GIRL WHO SAVED ME...
I CAN'T HELP HER...
BUT...
MAYBE M-MY ALTER-EGO CAAAAAAAOOOO--
AAAAOOOOOOOO
OH, THIS JUST KEEPS GETTING BETTER AND BETTER.
BUHOOM

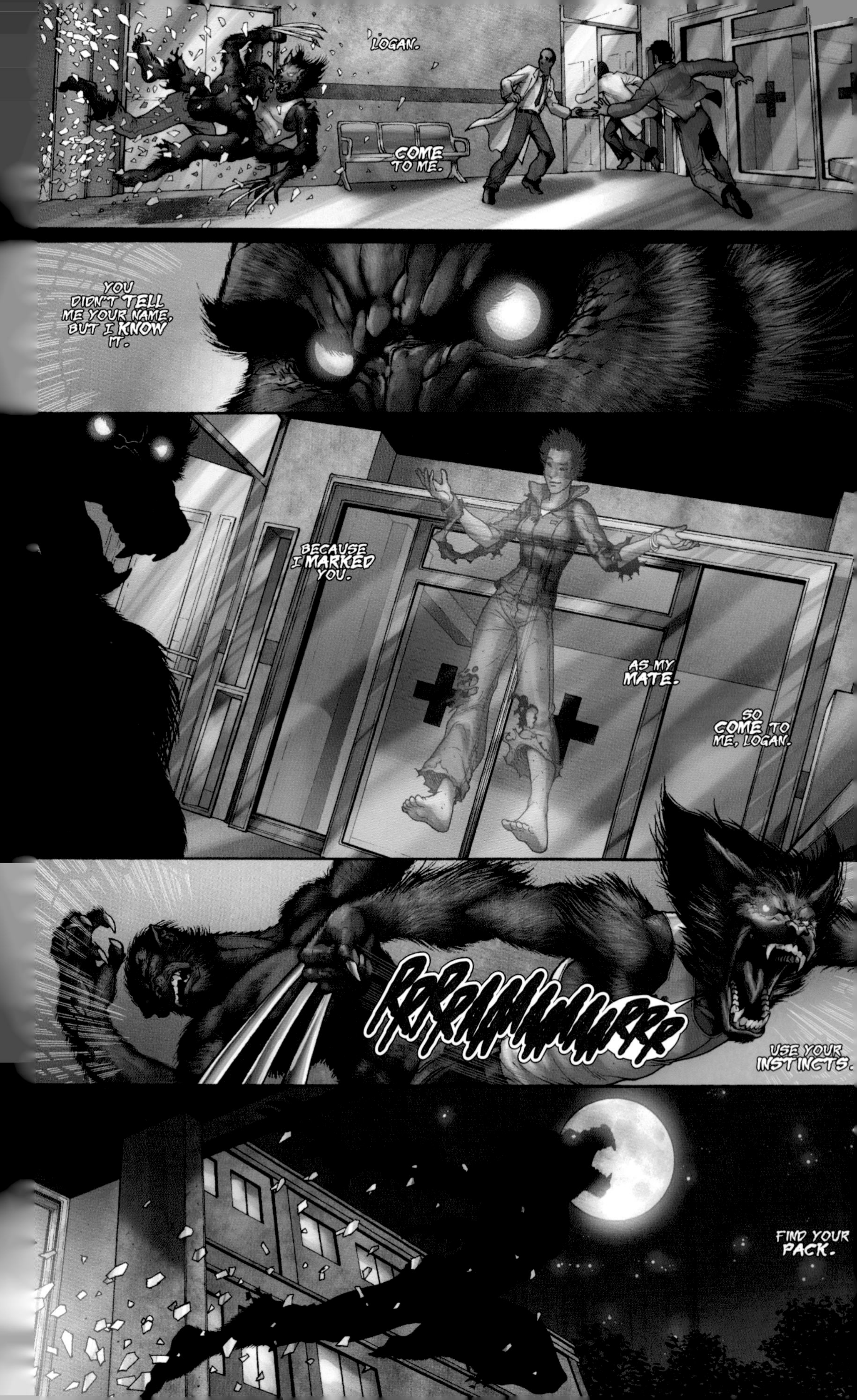
LOGAN.
COME TO ME.
YOU DIDN'T TELL ME YOUR NAME, BUT I KNOW IT.
BECAUSE I MARKED YOU.
AS MY MATE.
SO COME TO ME, LOGAN.
RRRRAAAAAAAAURRR
USE YOUR INSTINCTS.
FIND YOUR PACK.

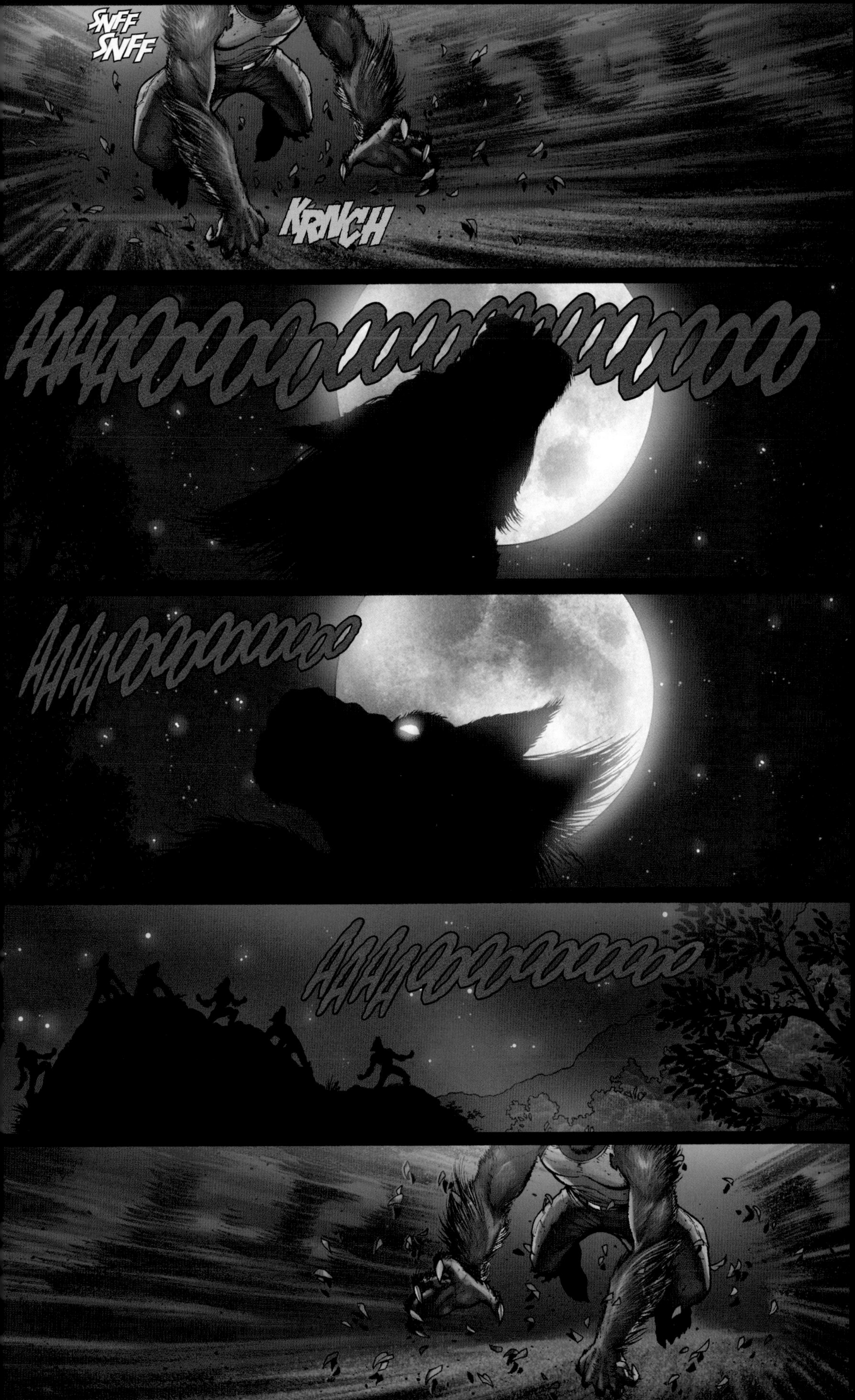
SNFF
SNFF
KRNCH
AAAOOOOOOOOOOOOOOOOOOOO
AAAOOOOOOOOOOOO
AAAOOOOOOOOOOOO

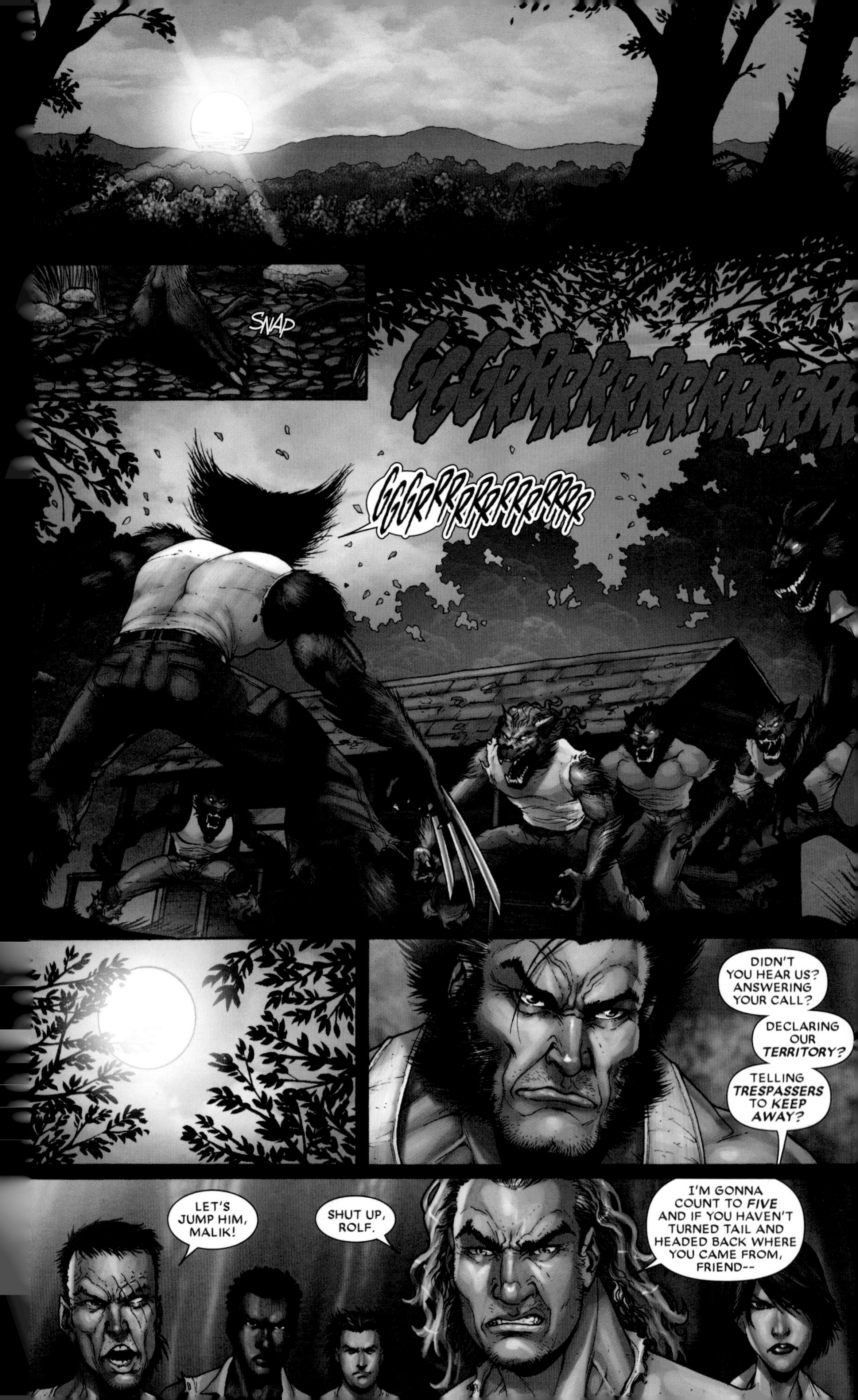
SNAP
GGGRRRRRRRRRRRRRRRRR
GGGRRRRRRRRRRRRR
DIDN'T YOU HEAR US? ANSWERING YOUR CALL?
DECLARING OUR TERRITORY?
TELLING TRESPASSERS TO KEEP AWAY?
LET'S JUMP HIM, MALIK!
SHUT UP, ROLF.
I'M GONNA COUNT TO FIVE AND IF YOU HAVEN'T TURNED TAIL AND HEADED BACK WHERE YOU CAME FROM, FRIEND--

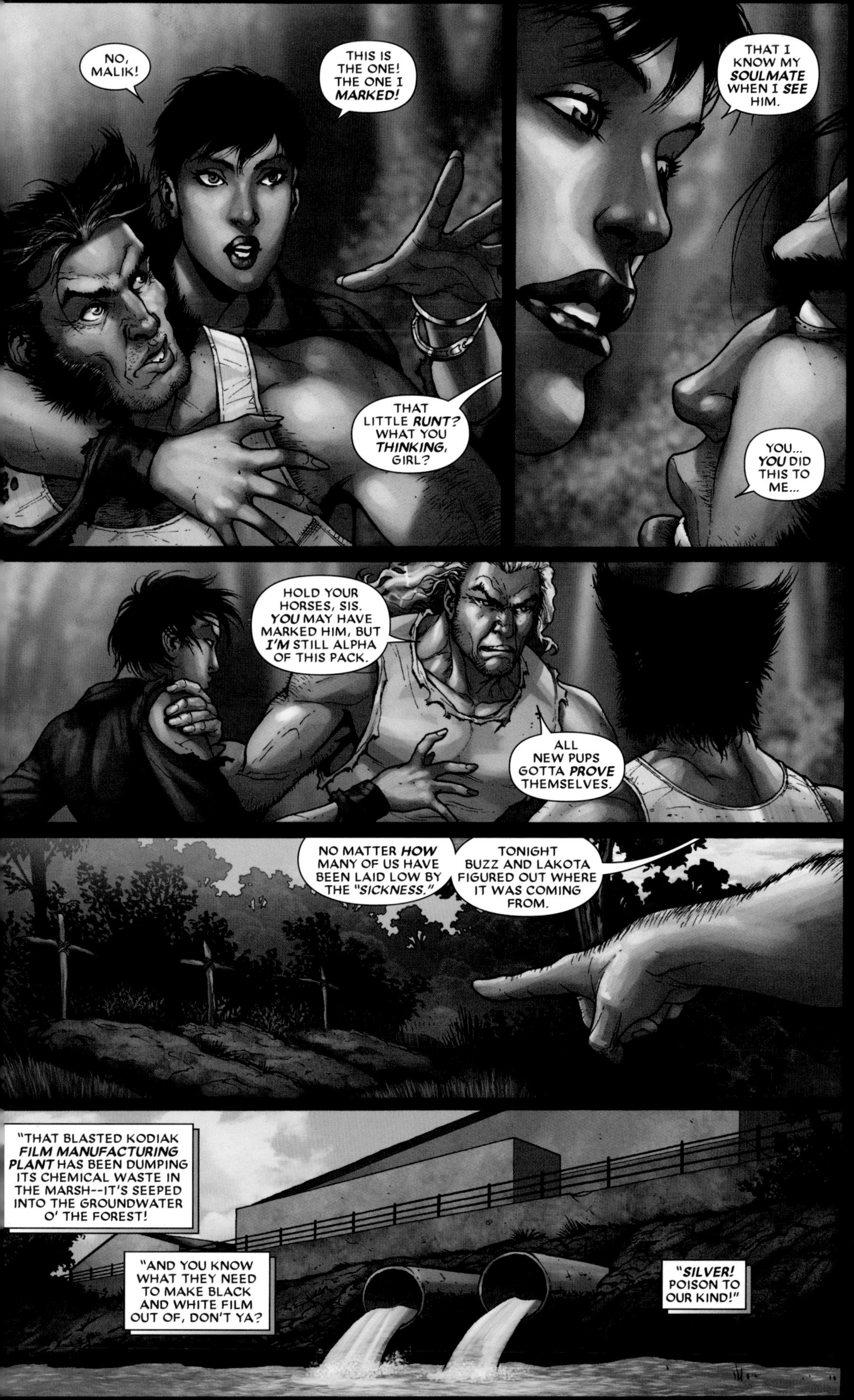
NO, MALIK!
THIS IS THE ONE! THE ONE I MARKED!
THAT LITTLE RUNT? WHAT YOU THINKING, GIRL?
THAT I KNOW MY SOULMATE WHEN I SEE HIM.
YOU... YOU DID THIS TO ME...
HOLD YOUR HORSES, SIS. YOU MAY HAVE MARKED HIM, BUT I'M STILL ALPHA OF THIS PACK.
ALL NEW PUPS GOTTA PROVE THEMSELVES.
NO MATTER HOW MANY OF US HAVE BEEN LAID LOW BY THE "SICKNESS."
TONIGHT BUZZ AND LAKOTA FIGURED OUT WHERE IT WAS COMING FROM.
"THAT BLASTED KODIAK FILM MANUFACTURING PLANT HAS BEEN DUMPING ITS CHEMICAL WASTE IN THE MARSH--IT'S SEEPED INTO THE GROUNDWATER O' THE FOREST!
"AND YOU KNOW WHAT THEY NEED TO MAKE BLACK AND WHITE FILM OUT OF, DON'T YA?
"SILVER! POISON TO OUR KIND!"

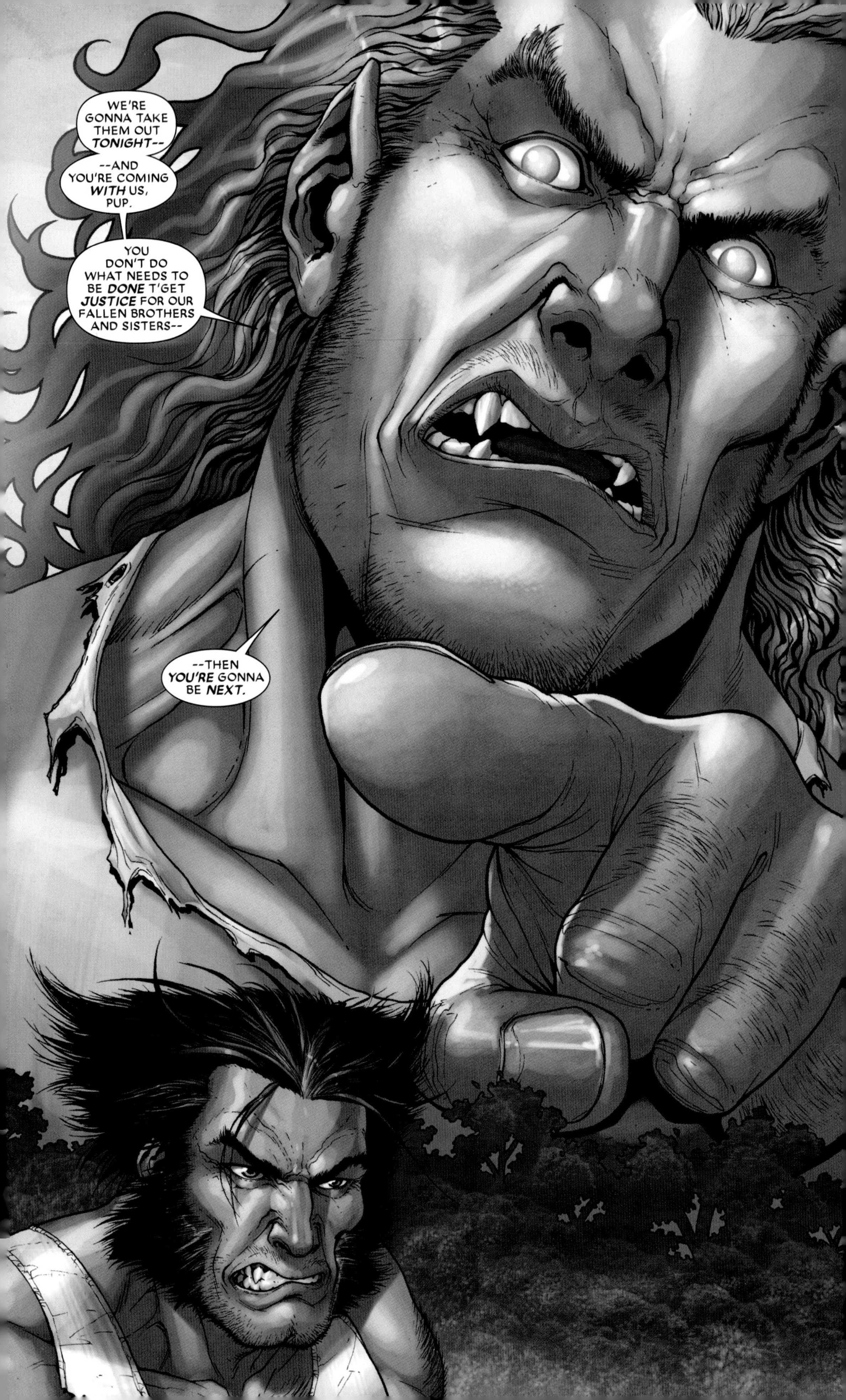
WE'RE GONNA TAKE THEM OUT TONIGHT--
--AND YOU'RE COMING WITH US, PUP.
YOU DON'T DO WHAT NEEDS TO BE DONE T'GET JUSTICE FOR OUR FALLEN BROTHERS AND SISTERS--
--THEN YOU'RE GONNA BE NEXT.